EARLY BIRD STORIES™

In the Den
&
Mick and Mom

Early★Reader

First American edition published in 2025 by Lerner Publishing Group, Inc.

An original concept by Elizabeth Dale

Illustrated by Giusi Capizzi

First published by Maverick Arts Publishing Limited

Licensed Edition
In the Den and Mick and Mom

Lerner Publications Company
An imprint of Lerner Publishing Group, Inc.
241 First Avenue North
Minneapolis, MN 55401 USA

For reading levels and more information, look up this title at www.lernerbooks.com.

Main body text set in Mikado. Typeface provided by HVD Fonts.

Library of Congress Cataloging-in-Publication Data

Names: Dale, Elizabeth, 1952–author. | Capizzi, Giusi, illustrator. | Dale, Elizabeth (Children's author). In the den. | Dale, Elizabeth (Children's author). Mick and Mom.
Title: In the den & Mick and Mom / Elizabeth Dale ; illustrated by Giusi Capizzi.
Other titles: In the den and Mick and Mom | Early reader. Red.
Description: First American edition. | Minneapolis : Lerner Publications , 2025. | Series: Early bird readers–red (early bird stories) | Audience: Ages 4–8. | Audience: Grades K–1. | Summary: In these two stories, kids play in a doghouse and Mom tries to keep the dog from splashing in puddles and fountains, but when it comes to bath time, Mick is not interested.
Identifiers: LCCN 2023051722 (print) | LCCN 2023051723 (ebook) | ISBN 9798765627112 (library binding) | ISBN 9798765628584 (paperback) | ISBN 9798765633045 (epub)
Subjects: LCSH: Readers (Primary) | Dogs—Juvenile fiction. | Doghouses—Juvenile fiction. | Baths—Juvenile fiction. | CYAC: Dogs—Fiction. | Doghouses—Fiction. | Baths—Fiction. | Humorous stories. | LCGFT: Readers (Publications) | Humorous fiction. | Picture books.
Classification: LCC PE1119.2 .D3448 2025 (print) | LCC PE1119.2 (ebook) | DDC 428.62 [E]—dc23/eng/20231107

LC record available at https://lccn.loc.gov/2023051722
LC ebook record available at https://lccn.loc.gov/2023051723

Manufactured in the United States of America
1-1010088-52096-12/7/2023

In the Den & Mick and Mom

Elizabeth Dale

Illustrated by
Giusi Capizzi

Lerner Publications ◆ Minneapolis

The Letter "N"

Trace the lower and upper case letter with a finger. Sound out the letter.

Down,
up,
around,
down

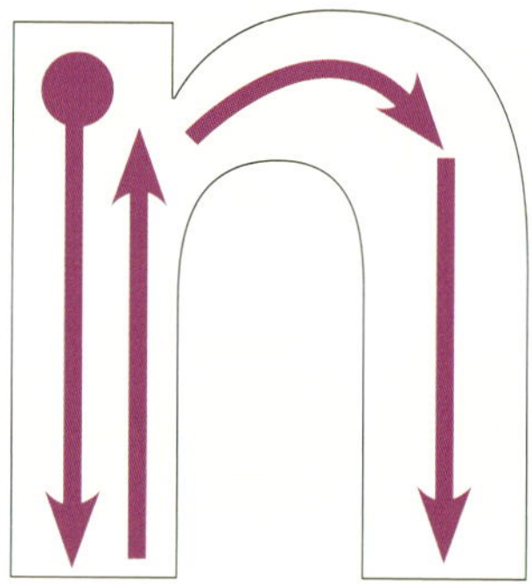

Up,
down,
up

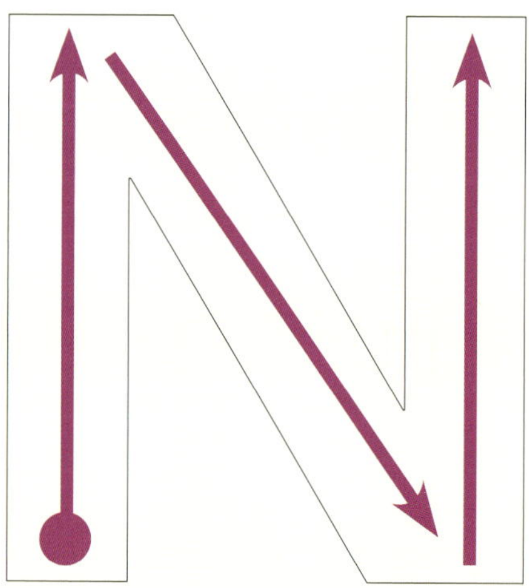

Some words to familiarize:

den

Meg

Mick

High-frequency words:

in a me is the
it no he his on of

Tips for Reading *In the Den*

- Practice the words listed above before reading the story.

- If the reader struggles with any of the other words, ask them to look for sounds they know in the word. Encourage them to sound out the words and help them read the words if necessary.

- After reading the story, ask the reader who the den belongs to.

Fun Activity

Build a den out of cardboard!

In the Den

Rob sits in a den.

Come in with me, Meg.
This den is big.
MICK

Meg sits in the den.

Come in with us, Tom.
It is fun.

Rob, Meg, and Tom sit in the den.

It is big! It is so much fun.

No! Do not come in the den, Mick!

But Mick comes in. He is big.
He wags his tail.

No, Mick, no!

Mick sits in his den . . .

. . . on top of
Rob and Meg
and Tom!

The Letter "M"

Trace the lower and upper case letter with a finger. Sound out the letter.

Down,
up, around,
down,
up, around,
down

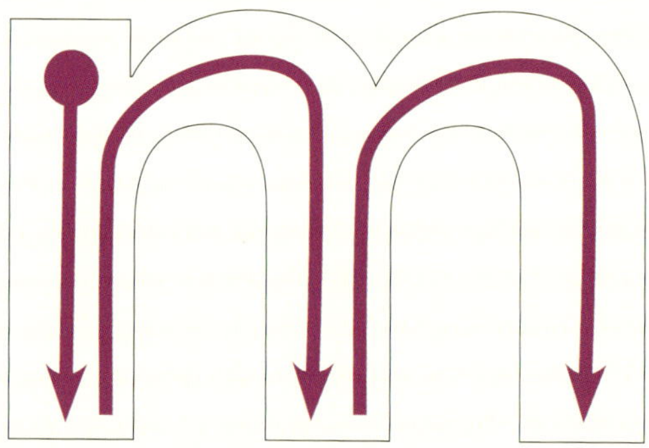

Up,
down,
up,
down

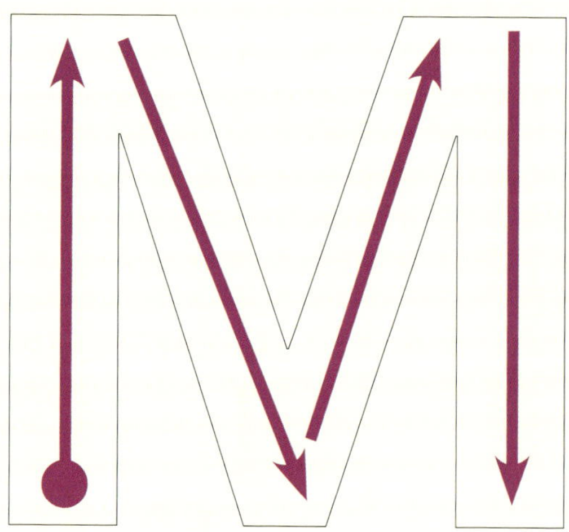

Some words to familiarize:

park

pond

tub

High-frequency words:

go to the no

Tips for Reading *Mick and Mom*

- Practice the words listed above before reading the story.

- If the reader struggles with any of the other words, ask them to look for sounds they know in the word. Encourage them to sound out the words and help them read the words if necessary.

- After reading the story, ask the reader why Mom wanted to get Mick wet.

Fun Activity

Draw another way Mick could get wet.

Mick and Mom

Mick and Mom go to the park.

Do not get wet, Mick!

Mick and Mom go to the store.
Do not get wet, Mick!

Mick and Mom go to the woods.

Do not get wet, Mick!

Mick and Mom go to the zoo.

Do not
get wet, Mick!

Mick and Mom go to the pond.

Do not get wet, Mick!

Mick and Mom go to the tub.

No!

COLOR	GRL
Silver	L-P
Gold	K-L
Purple	J-K
Orange	H-J
Green	G-I
Blue	E-G
Yellow	C-E
Red	C-D
Pink	A-C

Leveled for Guided Reading

Early Bird Stories have been edited and leveled by leading educational consultants to correspond with guided reading levels. The levels are assigned by taking into account the content, language style, layout, and phonics used in each book. Visit www.lernerbooks.com for more Early Bird Readers titles!

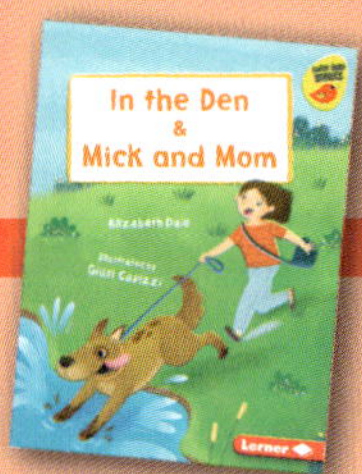